S H

HAUNTINGS

D1493969

" I was furious with Dad, and I was scared. Because when I opened the parcel, the exact moment I touched the picture, something weird happened. And my hands shook, my mouth went dry and my heart nearly leapt out of my body.

I saw a face in the glass – not my own face, round, red and angry, but someone else's – thin, pale, sad, with dark-brown hair. But my hair was blonde. It wasn't my reflection. "

HAUNTINGS

Mary Chapman

Ransom

SHADES 2.0
Hauntings
by Mary Chapman

Published by Ransom Publishing Ltd.
Radley House, 8 St. Cross Road, Winchester, Hampshire SO23 9HX, UK
www.ransom.co.uk

ISBN   978 178127 195 7
First published in 2008
This updated edition published by Ransom Publishing 2013

CONTENTS

ONE

Saturday, 3rd March. My birthday. Sitting round the kitchen table.

I'd opened all my cards and presents. I was feeling really flat.

Then Dad handed me a parcel.

'A little extra. Thought you might like it.'

It was scruffy, not even wrapped in proper birthday paper, just some creased, brown stuff.

Typical Dad. He might have made a bit more effort. My first birthday since Mum –

'Open it quick,' said Tom.

'I'll open it when I'm ready,' I snapped. 'Don't hassle me.'

'Come on, love,' said Gran, 'don't you want to see what it is?'

I shrugged.

'S'pose.'

I ripped off the brown paper. Underneath were several layers of newspaper. Inside was a picture. Except it wasn't really, not a proper one. Glass, a frame, and beneath the glass a grubby piece of cloth, sort of embroidered. Whatever was Dad thinking about, giving me this old junk?

Then my heart seemed to plunge down, and surge up again. Pounding. Thumping. The floor was moving. My legs were collapsing. The room swirled round. It was all blurry. Buzzing in my head. Was this what fainting was like? I'd never fainted in my life.

I took several deep breaths.

Tom was leaning on me.

'Let me look.'

'Don't – ' I pushed him away. 'Get off!'

Gran frowned.

I gripped the picture thing.

'What's the matter? Your hands are shaking,' said Tom.

'No, they're not.' I gave him another shove.

But he was right. *They were.* Not because I was in a temper, but because I was frightened.

'What do you think of it?' asked Dad.

' 's all right.'

'Don't you like it?'

'I said – it's all right.'

'You obviously don't like it.' His smile disappeared.

'Perhaps she doesn't know what it is, Jack?' said Gran. She always tried to keep the peace, but it wasn't easy. She'd moved in after Mum –

I knew what would happen, but I couldn't stop it. I stood up, pushed back my chair, shoved Tom out of the way. I didn't mean to hurt him, but he fell against the cooker, and started yelling. Typical.

I threw the picture down on to the table.

'I'm going to Sophie's.'

'Sit down!' Dad shouted.

'Let her go, Jack,' said Gran. 'She's upset.'

'She's upset? I'm upset. We're all upset!' Dad was still shouting.

I ran out of the room, slammed the front door behind me and headed up the road.

I was furious with Dad, and I was scared.

Because when I opened the parcel, the

exact moment I touched the picture, something weird happened. And my hands shook, my mouth went dry and my heart nearly leapt out of my body.

I saw a face in the glass – not my own face, round, red and angry, but someone else's – thin, pale, sad, with dark-brown hair. But my hair was blonde. It wasn't my reflection.

And something else. I *felt* different, as well as looking different. Usually I take breathing for granted. Don't notice I'm doing it. But every time I breathed in, I got a pain in my chest. It was a huge effort, just to take one breath at a time. I was exhausted and absolutely terrified.

I had to get away from all this. I was desperate to be somewhere ordinary and cheerful. Sophie's was the obvious place to go.

TWO

At first, I didn't say anything to Sophie about the face in the glass. If I told her, it would make it more real. Every now and again it flashed into my mind – that white face – but I blanked it out for as long as I could.

Sophie guessed there was something wrong though.

'What's up?' she said. 'You look a bit strange. I know you're sad about your mum, but there's something else, isn't there?'

So I told her everything that had happened that morning. For once, she didn't interrupt. When I'd finished, she said, 'Maybe you imagined it, because you're upset anyway. I'm sure it won't happen again.'

But she didn't sound sure, and she didn't convince me. Still, it was a relief to have told her. Maybe she was right, and I had imagined it after all.

'Can I stay here for the rest of the day, Sophs? I'd much rather be here than at home.'

'Yeah, 'course you can.'

'Is that all right with your gran?' Sophie's mum asked.

'Yeah. It's fine.'

We'd just started lunch when the phone rang. Sophie's mum answered it.

'Yes, she's here … She seems all right … ' I knew she was talking to Gran. She had that 'special' sympathetic voice adults used when they talked to me, or about me. They did it when Mum first got ill, and they still did. I wished they'd stop.

'I'm sorry. I didn't realise – she said it would be all right with you – I'll send her straight home.'

She put the phone down, frowning. 'That was your gran. She's expecting you home for your birthday lunch. You'd better go.'

'Sorry,' I mumbled.

'It's OK,' said Sophie. 'See you soon.'

But it wasn't OK. I liked Sophie's mum, and now she was annoyed with me as well. This was turning out to be a horrible birthday, even more horrible than I'd expected. Like Sophie said, it wasn't only about my birthday and Mum not being there. That was bad enough, but with the face appearing and then feeling so weird, I didn't want to go home in case it happened again.

THREE

Gran, Dad and Tom were sitting round the table, a nice, cosy threesome.

'And where do you think you've been?' asked Dad.

'Sophie's. I told you.'

'You didn't say you wouldn't be back for lunch,' said Dad. 'Your gran's cooked something special, and now it's ruined.'

'No it's not,' said Gran.

'It's so inconsiderate,' grumbled Dad.

'Come and sit down, love,' said Gran. 'It's your favourite – lasagne.'

'Well?' said Dad. 'Aren't you going to say thank you?'

'Thanks, Gran,' I muttered.

Actually it was good, but I wasn't going to say so, just because Dad had told me to – as if I was some little kid. Tom was rabbiting on, like he does. Gran was being *ever-so-interested*, at which she's the World Champion.

I know that sounds awful. I'm not a horrible person really. Gran was only doing her best. When I was being 'more mature' (as Dad put it) I could see it was difficult for her, leaving her own home, moving in with us, trying to keep things normal.

But mostly all I could think was that if Mum hadn't died, Gran wouldn't be there.

It was as if I thought Mum was dead
because Gran was there. I know that sounds
crazy. Maybe I *was* going crazy? Maybe that
was why I thought I'd seen that face?

Anyway, I didn't say a word, and neither
did Dad.

Until I stood up.

'Where do you think you're going now?'
he snapped.

'My room.'

'Then take that with you,' he said.

The picture was still on the worktop
where I'd left it, half-wrapped in crumpled,
brown paper.

'I don't want it,' I said. 'Who'd want a
present like that? It's rubbish!'

'How dare you!' Dad lunged forward over
the table and grabbed my wrist. I pulled
away.

'Jack!' Gran's voice was stern.

'Dad, stop it,' whimpered Tom.

'Calm down, both of you,' said Gran. 'Take it, love, and go up to your room for a bit.'

I grabbed the bundle.

Just as I was going out of the room, Dad said, 'Your mum wanted you to have that, you know.'

I ran upstairs. I wanted Mum, not this rubbishy old picture. Why on earth would Mum want me to have it? I didn't believe Dad. Not after what had happened this morning.

FOUR

I slammed my door and hurled the stupid present across the room. It smashed against the wall. There was a splintering sound.

'Good!'

I lay on my bed and started to cry. I'm not usually a weepy sort of person. Some birthday! Happy it certainly wasn't. My stomach felt empty. My head ached. My eyes were sore. My nose was all blocked up. I blew it hard, mopped my eyes and turned on my side.

'Oh, God!'

There was the picture, lying on the floor, probably smashed to pieces.

I remembered Dad's face when he gave me the parcel. He'd looked so pleased. Mum always said, 'It's the thought that counts.' My birthday was the first one in our family since she died. It was Mum who always did birthdays, presents and stuff. This was a first for Dad. What if it was true – that Mum wanted me to have this? And I'd broken it.

Maybe I could mend it. Nobody would know. I'd go downstairs, say sorry and it'd be all right. Dad and I are both fiery, but we don't hold grudges and we don't sulk.

But when I picked the picture up, slivers

of glass fell out and the frame nearly came apart. I felt relieved at first. There couldn't be any reflections of someone else's face if there was no glass. But breaking it actually made matters much worse. Dad was going to be even angrier now.

Still, perhaps if I took all the glass out, I could stick the frame together and nobody'd notice? Where the frame had splintered, the sticky paper on the back had come away. I pulled at a corner. It was brittle, sort of powdery, and tore away easily. Might as well take it all off. I pulled at the jagged strip. Underneath were some little nails, holding an oblong of wood in place. I tried to pull them out, but they were so rusty they just snapped off. I lifted the piece of wood out. Now I could see the back of the embroidered thing, a dirty-grey colour. And almost stuck to it was a sheet of yellowish paper with marks on it.

Carefully, I peeled it away. I held it up to the light. The marks were handwriting, spidery and old-fashioned. Some of it so faded that I could hardly make it out.

This was what it said:

> Rebecca Jane Chantry
>
> Finished 11th January, 1858
>
> At Mrs Addison's School,
>
> Church Street, Lincoln

The paper fluttered from my fingers.

My legs went all wobbly again. I had to sit down on the bed. Everything was moving, just like it did downstairs, whirling round, and the room went dark. My heart was thudding away like anything.

You see, that's *my* name – Rebecca Jane Chantry.

FIVE

It didn't make sense.

I must have made a mistake.

But the words were there, just the same.

Below was a funny little drawing, rather like something Tom would draw. It was a girl in old-fashioned clothes. The drawing was smudgy, but she seemed to be holding a piece of paper with some words written on it:

Rebecca Chantry 1858

Underneath the drawing were more words:

Rebecca bringing home her sampler

Sampler? Whatever was that? Was it that scrappy, old bit of embroidery? I looked at it again. There, at the bottom, was the name again:

Rebecca Jane Chantry

Dizzy. Must sit down.

Rebecca Chantry. Rebecca, Rebecca … Voices calling. That buzzing in my head again. Felt floaty. Strange smell – a mixture of dust, chalk, wet soot. More voices, children singing? Not proper singing though, it was all on the same note, like chanting. Then it faded, and that aching pain in my chest came back.

I wish the coughing would stop, but it won't. I feel so sick and faint. Rebecca. Rebecca …

'Rebecca! Rebecca! Tea-time!'

Almost dark. Don't know how long I'd been sitting there, in a daze. Don't know what time it was. No idea. Hands stiff and cold with gripping this sampler thing.

Gran was calling me. That's what woke me out of my day-dream, though it was more like a nightmare.

'Rebecca!'

She was knocking at the door.

'Rebecca!'

I ran to the door and shouted, 'I'm coming!'

I didn't want her bursting in, finding me sitting in the dark in a trance. I dashed back to the bed, grabbed everything and stuffed it all under the duvet. I was breathing fast. My heart was pounding away again. So I took several deep breaths, then opened the door and went downstairs.

SIX

Cake and candles.

Somehow, I got through my birthday tea.
Nobody said anything about the present,
and I tried not to think about it. I managed
to be polite to Dad and not snap at Tom,
though he was even more irritating than
usual.

When Tom went to bed, Gran followed

him upstairs to make sure he cleaned his teeth properly, so it was just Dad and me, half-watching some comedy programme on TV. I kept trying out sentences in my head, but I couldn't say them. I wanted to say 'sorry', but that wouldn't come out either. And Dad seemed to be staying clear of anything to do with my birthday.

Then he picked up the newspaper. I kept on staring at the screen. Every time Dad turned a page, the paper rattled. I couldn't bear it. Eventually I gabbled, 'Headache. Going to bed.'

I knew Dad wouldn't ask any questions. Headaches, tummy pains – he leaves all that to Gran – women's stuff. So he just nodded and turned back to his paper.

Gran was still with Tom, so I shouted goodnight and dived into my room. I was desperately hoping I'd got it wrong, that it wasn't my name after all. I could easily have misread it. I took the picture and the sheet of paper over to the window. But there was no mistake. It definitely said,

Rebecca Jane Chantry.

My name.

I looked at the embroidery more closely: rows of letters of the alphabet and numbers, a border of red blobs. Except for the red and the green, the colours had faded. It all looked rather scruffy. I don't know much about embroidery, but it looked like cross-stitch. Mum used to do that. She tried to teach me, but soon gave up because I was hopeless. I got so fed up I threw my tray-cloth across the room. Mum laughed and said there was no point trying to teach a cross-patch to cross-stitch.

Thinking of Mum, I got a lump in my throat. The embroidered letters and numbers went all blurry, the reds and greens swirling about. That dizzy feeling was coming back. I'd better do something, quick.

I switched on my computer and put 'sampler' into Google. Loads of stuff came up. I clicked on one or two websites. One of them said that Victorian girls had to embroider samplers to practise different kinds of stitches, so they could be good wives in the future. Poor things! Is that what Rebecca Jane was doing? I'd rather do SATS than sew a sampler.

How bored she must have been, embroidering letters and numbers, having to unpick every mistake. The border was pretty, though. I hoped she enjoyed doing that. When I thought of her as just an ordinary schoolgirl, I didn't feel so scared.

It was getting dark. I'd light the candle

Sophie gave me for my birthday. Gran'd go mad if she knew, but I didn't care.

'We'll be burned to death in our beds!' she'd say.

The room looked cosy in the flickering candlelight. I settled back on the bed and studied the sampler again. It was strange; the candlelight seemed to make the colours more vivid. I could see pinks, blues and yellows now. I shivered. Dad must have turned the central heating off early again. I wish he wouldn't. It was really cold. I shuddered.

Pictures in my mind. Rebecca Jane at school in winter, bending low over her sewing in the dim light ...

SEVEN

It's icy cold in the schoolroom. I rub my hands together, but I can't get them warm. Hard, wooden bench; feet numb with cold in my boots. I'm so tired from sewing. I'm always tired. My head hurts, my eyes are sore, my neck's stiff. I've a pain in my chest. It's hard to breathe. My fingers ache. The middle finger of my left hand is so sore. I must have pricked it

again with my needle. I'm always doing that.
It's hard to see on these dull, winter afternoons.
The tips of my fingers are all rough. Mother
says I need to be more careful. There's a drop
of blood on the tip. Bright, shiny red, it oozes
out and, before I can do anything, it drips on to
the sampler, just below the R of Rebecca. I
could cry. I've nearly finished it at last, after all
these weeks, and now I've spoilt it, but I
mustn't cry, I mustn't give up …

… The candle sputtered and went out.

I'd been in some sort of daze again. Only this time I'd gone a long way away, and a long time ago.

I jumped off the bed and ran to switch on the light. I was still shivering. I put my hand on the radiator. It was burning hot, so hot that I snatched my hand away. But why was I so cold?

I must have fallen asleep. A dream?

Fragments came back to me, the way dreams do. Sore fingers? A drop of blood? I looked down at my fingertips. They were perfectly smooth and silky. No blood, not a scratch.

I lay the sampler on my desk and flattened it out. At the bottom, beside the name, was her age and the date:

Rebecca Jane Chantry, aged 11 years 1858.

I looked more closely. There was a faded, brownish stain, just below the R of Rebecca – *just below the R of Rebecca …*

The words seemed familiar, as if I'd thought them before. How could I? I hadn't seen this sampler until today. Or had I ?

… blood … Bright, shiny red … drips onto the sampler …

Stop it, I told myself. I must have noticed the stain *before* I had that strange dream.

Then it got into the dream, the way

things do, and got all muddled up. This was a perfectly ordinary piece of embroidery. But I knew it wasn't, and I knew I hadn't seen the stain before.

I needed to find out more about the sampler. Where did Dad get it? I had to stop thinking about those spooky dreams, put them right out of my mind. Maybe Rebecca Jane was my great-great-grandmother or something? And that was why Mum wanted me to have the sampler. I'd ask Dad first thing tomorrow.

EIGHT

We always had a late breakfast on Sundays. Dad usually did a fry-up.

'How's the headache?' he asked, turning the bacon over.

'What? Oh, all right,' I said.

Actually, I had a real headache now. I'd hardly slept. When I did, my dreams were a jumble of voices, faces.

'Full English?'

'Er. Yeah, OK. Sorry, about yesterday,' I mumbled.

'It's all right,' he said. 'Sorry I got a bit stressed. Now, tuck into that.'

I was washing up and Dad was drying. It seemed a good time to talk.

'Is the sampler a family heirloom?' I asked. 'Is that why Mum wanted me to have it?'

'Afraid not,' he said. 'I found it in a junk shop, not long after we knew your mum was pregnant with you. I had to buy it, with the name being Chantry. I know it's a common name round here, but it was such a coincidence.'

He grinned.

'We'd nearly had our first, big row, about the baby's name. We'd decided on Thomas for a boy, but we couldn't agree on a girl's name. I wanted Sarah Jane, after her, but she wanted Marianne, after some character in a book. I thought that was too fancy. Neither of us would give in.'

I imagined a much younger Mum and Dad, squabbling, a bit like me and Tom, their lives in front of them, all sorts of hopes and plans.

'Who won in the end?' I asked.

'Neither of us,' said Dad. 'Eventually your mum said, let's call her Rebecca, after the girl who made the sampler. And I said, might as well make it Rebecca Jane, so at least she'll have your second name. So we both got our own way.'

I'd never known about any of this.

'We meant to get the sampler cleaned and re-framed,' said Dad, 'but we couldn't afford to. So it was put away in a drawer for years. Then we moved house, and your mum got ill soon after. A lot of stuff was just left in boxes, and we forgot all about it. Then she was better for a while, so we started unpacking and found the sampler. Mum said we must get it framed and give it to you. You'd be old enough to appreciate it now.'

I felt I'd let Mum down, because I hadn't appreciated it.

'She was upset because I didn't get round to doing it,' said Dad. 'She wanted to give it to you herself, but she got ill again, and then – I wish I'd done it properly, like she wanted, and had it re-framed for you.'

'It's as well you didn't,' I said.

'What d'you mean?'

So I told him about the drawing I'd found. But I didn't tell him the rest.

NINE

I flopped onto my bed and lay there with my eyes closed, thinking about Dad and Mum before I was born. I smiled, imagining how Rebecca Jane helped them agree on my name. I was sorry we weren't related, but I still wanted to know more about her. My eyes closed. Must get up in a minute and do my Maths, and there was that

French as well. Just a few more minutes, then I –

Oh, such a pain in my chest. Coughing. Can't stop. Specks of red on my handkerchief. Can't get my breath. Hurts when I breathe in. Must try. In. Out. In. Out. The pain's easing now …

I sat up, gasping.

What was happening to me? Was this a heart attack? People my age don't have heart attacks – do they? My breathing wasn't right. I tried to slow it down. Gradually, I got it back to normal. But I still felt strange, as though I wasn't really there. I felt hot and feverish, all cold and shivery, like when I've got a temperature. My head felt fuzzy.

My room didn't seem like mine any more. It had all my stuff in it, the colours I'd chosen. But everything seemed too bright.

It was like someone else's room, a stranger's. I was just a visitor.

It was like when Mum first died. I was in a sort of bubble, cut off from everyone else. Nothing seemed real. I couldn't believe any of it was happening. I kept thinking I was going to wake up. But of course I didn't. Eventually, things went back to sort-of normal.

But now those weird feelings were back. Dad, Tom and Gran, even Sophie, didn't seem as real as Rebecca Jane. I didn't feel real myself.

I got off the bed and went over to my mirror. I wanted to make sure I was still there. I remember doing that after Mum died – staring for ages at my own reflection, thinking I looked the same as I had before, but knowing I wasn't, not inside. I never would be again. My life had changed for ever.

But looking in the mirror didn't help. The face that stared back at me wasn't mine. It was the one I saw in the glass yesterday. Thin, pale, framed by long, dark hair. So pale I could almost see through it.

I *could* see through it, to my own round face, much paler than normal, but nothing like as ghostly-white. I opened my mouth to scream, but no sound came, just like in nightmares when you try to shout for help, but you can't even make a squeak. I'd never been so scared in my life. I stared at the mirror, petrified that the other face would return.

And it did. My face dissolved again, and that white face reappeared. Bright, feverish eyes stared out at me. Dark shadows beneath them. The girl before me raised her arm. Slowly and painfully, the arm moved up and down as she brushed her long, dark hair …

I feel so tired. My cough kept me awake all last night. Mother sat up with me. She said I had a fever. But I must go back to school and finish my sampler. Mother would be so pleased if I did. My breathing's better tonight, so maybe I'll sleep. Then tomorrow I'll feel refreshed. I'll go to school and in the afternoon I'll embroider my name, and then my sampler will be complete. I can bring it home at last, like all the other girls did at the end of the Christmas term. I'm so weary. Brushing my hair makes the pain in my chest worse. Just a few more strokes. I want my hair to shine, like other girls' hair …

The girl in the mirror put down the brush and stretched out her hands towards me. I shrank back.

I could see my own face again, and my arm held above my head, my hand a fist, as if I was gripping something. I lowered my arm, unclenched my fist and looked over my shoulder. There was nobody behind me.

She was taking over my body, taking over my life. I was weak and frail. I wasn't myself any more. I had to get back to the present. I didn't want to be trapped in the past.

TEN

'You've got to get a grip, girl!' I said out loud, and pinched myself hard, several times, on both arms. My nails left marks, like half-moons.

What else could I do to get myself back into the present?

Maths homework, like pinching myself, a painful way of remembering I was Rebecca

Chantry, living in the twenty-first century.

I did as much Maths as I could, and then I had a go at the French. It was so totally boring. I started to feel just a little bit more normal. I could hear sounds from downstairs – the TV, a door banging, Gran clattering in the kitchen. Maybe I'd dreamt all that mirror stuff?

No, I knew I hadn't.

I ought to mend the sampler. I could easily stick the frame together with glue, and fix cardboard across the back to hold it all together.

It was then I realised, as I picked up the drawing, that it wasn't a single sheet of paper after all. It was folded over.

I opened it. There were just a few words written inside.

14th March 1858, Rebecca Jane, beloved daughter of Samuel and

Charlotte Chantry, died aged 11 years

I couldn't believe it. I'd wanted to know more about Rebecca Jane, but I didn't want to know she'd died so young.

I could see she wasn't much good at drawing, and she wasn't brilliant at needlework either, but she didn't give up. She stuck at things, even if they were boring, even if they were a struggle. She'd died only a couple of months after finishing her sampler. Was she already ill when she was sewing it?

Something had happened when I was holding the sampler. What was it?

… a pain in my chest. Coughing. Can't stop. Specks of red on my handkerchief. Can't get my breath. Hurts when I breathe in. Must try. In. Out. In. Out. The pain's easing now …

What an effort it would have been, sitting in a cold schoolroom, feeling so ill, struggling to sew a stupid sampler, practising to be the good wife she would never live to be.

She was younger than me. She'd had such a short life, even shorter than Mum's. It wasn't fair.

And what about my life? When I'd looked in the mirror and seen the girl, Rebecca Jane, I'd felt that I was her, that she was in my body.

I rang Sophie and told her what I'd found.

'That's so sad,' she said.

'Yeah, I know. And it's scary.'

'Why?'

So then I told her absolutely everything.

'When did you say she'd died?' asked Sophie.

'14th March 1858,' I said. 'It's the fourth today, so in ten days' time it'll be the anniversary – exactly one hundred and fifty years ago.'

'I'm sure that doesn't mean anything,' said Sophie.

But she said it too quickly. I wasn't reassured.

'I don't like it, Sophs,' I said. 'It's spooking me. I think Rebecca Jane is trying to take over my body, swap lives, so she can live mine and I'll end up with hers. But that's not a life. It's death.'

'Stop it, Becks!' Sophie sounded angry and scared. 'That's horror film stuff.' I thought she was going to put the phone down.

'I'm sorry,' I said. 'I didn't mean to scare you. I know this sounds awful, but I've got to get rid of that sampler, before the anniversary. Otherwise it's going to keep dragging me back into the past.'

'But won't your Dad wonder where it is?'

'Yeah, I s'pose so.'

'Listen, Becks, it's late. We can't think straight. Let's talk about it tomorrow. Is there somewhere you can put the sampler tonight, so at least it's not in your room?'

I thought for a moment.

'I know. I'll put it in the cupboard on the landing. After all, it's been somewhere in the house for years. I just haven't known about it. And I guess she hasn't known about me.'

'That's a good idea.' Sophie sounded relieved. 'See you tomorrow.'

I felt better for a while, having told Sophie everything, but I soon got that empty feeling in my stomach again. I bundled up the sampler and frame and everything, crept out of my room and stuffed the lot into the bottom of the landing cupboard.

I felt so confused. In a way, I didn't want to throw the sampler away. It reminded me of Mum, and she'd wanted me to have it. It was like an extra present from her. And I felt sorry for Rebecca Jane, that poor, little girl. The sampler was all that was left of her life. But I didn't want to be haunted forever. I wanted my life back.

ELEVEN

I couldn't sleep. Actually, I daren't go to sleep, in case I died in the night. I couldn't get thoughts of death out of my mind . Rebecca Jane died young, and so would I. *That's* what it all meant. That's what she wanted. I was convinced of it now. I was going to die on the anniversary of Rebecca Jane's death, if not before.

But I must have drifted off. I opened my eyes to thick darkness.

… I feel hot, sweating, then cold and shivery. Pains in my chest. The coughing starts. Can't breathe. Struggle to sit up – coughing, gasping for air. It goes on and on. At last, I fall back onto the pillow. My eyes close. I'm so tired. A cool hand on my forehead, gently stroking. Mother …

… Mum?

Darkness.

I opened my eyes. The street light shone through the curtains.

I sat up, remembering. Why was it so dark before? My room was never completely dark. Had the street light gone off, or had something else happened? Someone had been there, beside my bed. Who was it? Who was I?

I turned on the light and reached for my

mobile. I'd ring Sophie. No, mustn't. I was being stupid, panicking about nothing. It was just my imagination. *Too much imagination for your own good*, Gran said. I lay down again, still holding my mobile tight, fixed my eyes on the gap between the curtains. Waited for morning.

'You must be psychic,' said Sophie.

It was break. We were in the Art Room. There were no other kids there. We'd asked Miss Hall if we could stay in to finish our projects.

'Yes,' she said, and then she stared at me. 'You're looking very pale, Rebecca. Dark circles under your eyes. Are you all right?'

'I'm OK, thanks,' I said. 'Just a bit tired.'

'Where's the sampler?' asked Sophie, when Miss Hall had gone.

'Still in the cupboard,' I said. 'I feel bad

about that, shutting Rebecca Jane away in a cupboard.'

'She's been shut away somewhere for years,' said Sophie. 'It's no different.'

'No, but – I know this sounds weird – I just wonder if, now she's been found again, she's haunting me, because she's been neglected for so long, hidden away. Nobody knowing about her, or her life.'

Sophie gave me one of her looks.

'Have you lost it, Becks?'

'No!'

'If you're right,' said Sophie, 'which I don't think you are for one minute, but if you are, what do you do about it? You can't go on being haunted like this, or whatever it is. If you've not lost it already, you soon will.'

'Thanks!' I snapped. 'That's really helpful.'

'I'm worried about you,' said Sophie. 'All

this on top of your mum dying. It's too much.'

She was right.

'You're not to tell anybody,' I said.

'I won't say anything – yet. But if you keep having those trances, or whatever, then I shall tell your gran. She could take you to the doctor's.'

'Sophie! What are you saying? I'm not going crazy.'

She'd voiced one of my own worst fears. I didn't want to hear it.

'I know, but – '

At that moment Miss Hall bustled in.

'Come on, you two, time to clear up. Then go outside for five minutes. The fresh air'll do you good, Rebecca.'

For the rest of the day I couldn't stop thinking about what I should do. Every time I glanced in Sophie's direction she was staring at me, a puzzled frown on her face. I knew she was worried. She just didn't want to let on that she was. That's why she was being so argumentative.

We didn't have time to talk again until we were on our way home.

'I've decided what I'm going to do,' I said.

'What?'

'I'm going to ask Dad to get the sampler, and the drawing, framed properly.'

'And?'

'That's it.'

'What's the point of that?' asked Sophie.

'I think that if we find a place in our home for Rebecca, and she's not hidden away, she'll know she's not forgotten,' I said. 'Then she won't need to come back and try to get inside my skin, or drag me back into the past, or make me die like her, so she's not alone. What do you think?'

'It's worth a try, I s'pose,' said Sophie.

'You could be a bit more encouraging,' I said.

'Sorry, I feel out of my depth.'

That scared me. Sophie was usually so confident.

'But you've got to do something,' she said. 'And there's just a chance it might work.'

To tell the truth, I didn't feel at all hopeful either.

TWELVE

After Tom had gone to bed, I showed Dad and Gran the piece of paper about Rebecca Jane's death.

'Oh, love,' Dad said, 'I didn't want my present to make you sad.'

'I want to make sure we don't forget her,' I said, and told them my idea. But I still didn't tell them the whole story behind it.

'Tomorrow lunchtime I'll take the sampler and the drawing to that shop on the corner of Oak Street,' said Dad. 'Get them framed properly, like your mum wanted.'

I was horrified when Dad came home and said it would be a whole week before they were ready. Tomorrow was the sixth of March. That meant they wouldn't be ready until the thirteenth of March, only one day before the anniversary. What if they still weren't ready then? What would happen to me?

How was I going to get through the next week? Even though the sampler was out of the house, I was terrified of being on my own, being haunted – day or night. I spent as much time as I could round Sophie's, when I wasn't at school.

One day Miss Hall took me on one side and said, 'Rebecca, are you sure there's nothing wrong ? You look very thin. In fact, you don't look yourself at all.'

I felt like saying she was right. I wasn't myself. In fact, I didn't know whose self I was. But I just mumbled something about an upset stomach, and the bell rang so I escaped.

At home in the evenings I stayed downstairs – even played games with Tom – and watched TV with Dad and Gran until it was time for bed. Then I read for as long as I could, trying not to fall asleep. Eventually though, I did, but I kept waking up all the time. It was like I had to be on guard.

'You look terrible,' said Sophie.

'I feel terrible,' I said.

The following Tuesday evening, Dad

came home from work with a parcel.

'You unwrap it,' he said. 'It's your present, after all.'

My hands were all damp and clammy. I wiped them on my jeans, then folded back the tissue paper.

The sampler was simply framed in plain, dark wood. Although the colours were still faded, somehow they seemed to glow. The drawing was in a smaller, matching frame.

I hugged Dad.

'Thanks. It's a great birthday present.'

Gran looked relieved, and Dad beamed.

'It's weird,' I said. 'I wouldn't be me if it wasn't for you and Mum, and my name wouldn't be Rebecca Jane if it wasn't for the sampler. Even though she's not related, she is part of this family. This is where she belongs.'

I went up to my room to hang the

sampler and the drawing side by side.

There you are, Rebecca Jane,' I said. 'You won't be forgotten now.'

Every day, for weeks afterwards, Sophie asked me,

'Any hauntings?'

'No.'

Then one day I said, 'You don't need to keep asking me. I was right, wasn't I? Somehow, and I don't know how, Rebecca Jane realises she's not forgotten. So the bad things that happened to her – being ill and dying and all that – don't get into my head any more. She's found her place, here – with us, and I can live my own life again.'